DATE DUE

WE CAN READ about NATURE!™

IF GRASS COULD TALK

by ANITA HOLMES

BENCHMARK **B**OOKS

MARSHALL CAVENDISH
NEW YORK

With thanks to
Susan Jefferson, first grade teacher at Miamitown
Elementary, Ohio, for sharing her innovative teaching
techniques in the Fun with Phonics section.

Benchmark Books
Marshall Cavendish Corporation
99 White Plains Road
Tarrytown, New York 10591

Text copyright © 2001 by Marshall Cavendish

Photo research by Candlepants, Inc.

Cover photo: *Photo Researchers, Inc.* / M. P. Kahl

The photographs in this book are used by permission and through the courtesy of:
Animals, Animals / Earth Scenes: Nancy Rotenberg, 4; Leonard L. T. Rhodes, 5; Charles
Palek6 (middle); Carson Baldwin Jr., 11 (top left); Leonard Lee Rue III, 11 (top right);
Nigel J. H.Smith, 15; Jack Wilburn, 17; Victoria McCormick, 24-25. *Photo Researchers,
Inc.:* MichaelLustbader, 5; Alan L. Detrick 6 (top); Kenneth W. Fink, 6 (bottom); K. G.
Vock / OKAPIA, 9(bottom); Garry D. McMichael, 10; Noble Proctor, 11 (bottom left); J.
F. Lanzarone /HOAQUI, Jeff Apoian, 13; Joyce Photographics, 14; Kenneth Murrary, 16
(top); Alan D.Carey, 20; Nigel J. Dennis, 21; Earl Roberge, 27 (top); Jerry Wachter, 27
(bottom); NigelCattlin, 29. *Animals, Animals:* Klaus-Peter Wolf, 8; George Bernard, 9
(top); E. R. Degginger,22 (bottom); Patti Murray, 23; Joe McDonarld, 26. *Corbis:*
Nevada Wier, 16 (bottom);Macduff Everton, 18; Albrecht G. Schaefer, 19; Annie Griffiths
Belt, 28.

Library of Congress Cataloging-in-Publication Data

Holmes, Anita, date
If grass could talk / by Anita Holmes
p. cm.– (We can read about nature!)
Includes index (p.32).
Summary: Grasses describe the important jobs that they do, from feeding animals and
grain harvesting to making reed furniture and beautifying gardens.
ISBN 0-7614-1111-9
1.Grasses—Juvenile literature. 2. Grain—Juvenile literature. 3. Grasses—Utilization—
Juvenile literature. [1. Grasses.] I. Title
QK495.G74H66 2001   584'.9—dc21   99-088056

Printed in Italy

1 3 5 6 4 2

Look for us inside this book.

bamboo
barley
corn
oats
reeds
rice
rye
sugarcane
wheat

The world is full of grasses.
They can grow almost anywhere.

Grass in a mountain stream

Grasses on a lava flow in Hawaii

Grass comes in many
sizes, shapes, and colors—

soft and short . . .

thick and red . . .

thin and green . . .

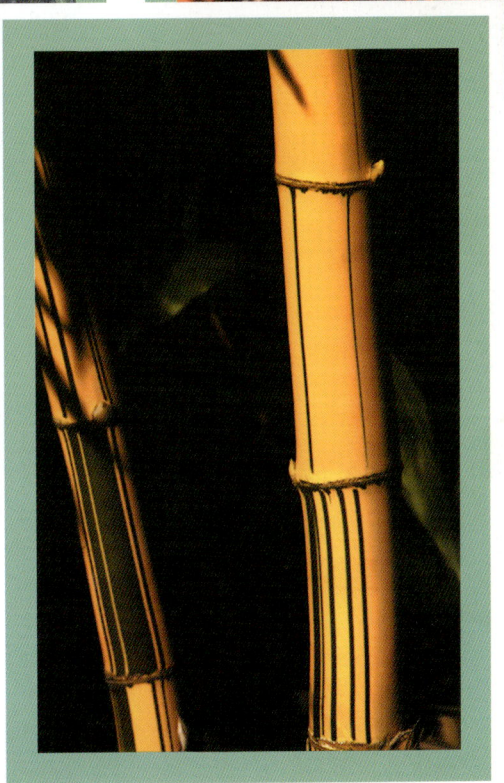

tall, striped,
and hollow.

If grass could talk, it would say, we grow in fields and meadows. We are food for sheep and cows and horses.

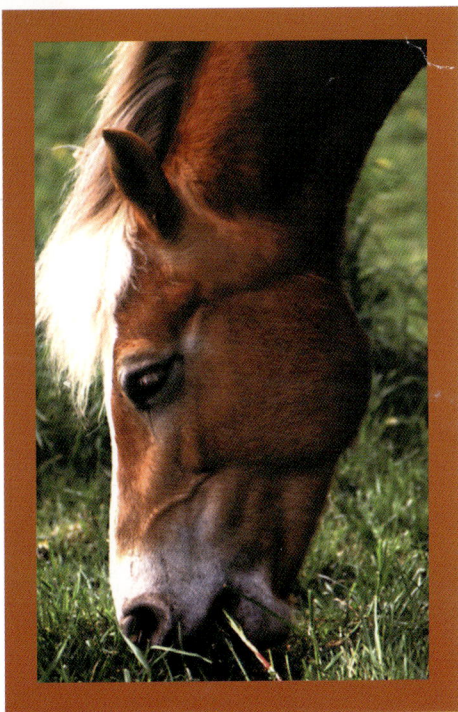

We are grasses called cereals.

Corn

Oats

Rice

Rye

Barley

11

Farmers harvest our grains.
People and animals eat us.

Wheat

We are called sugarcane.
We grow where it is hot
and there is plenty of water.

We taste sweet.
People make sugar from sugarcane.

People turn us into wonderful objects.

A girl collects reeds in Peru.

A woman weaves baskets from bamboo in Vietnam.

A scarecrow guards a field
in California.

People make houses of grass,

from Iceland . . .

to the Philippines.

Animals build nests with us.

Baby cottontails

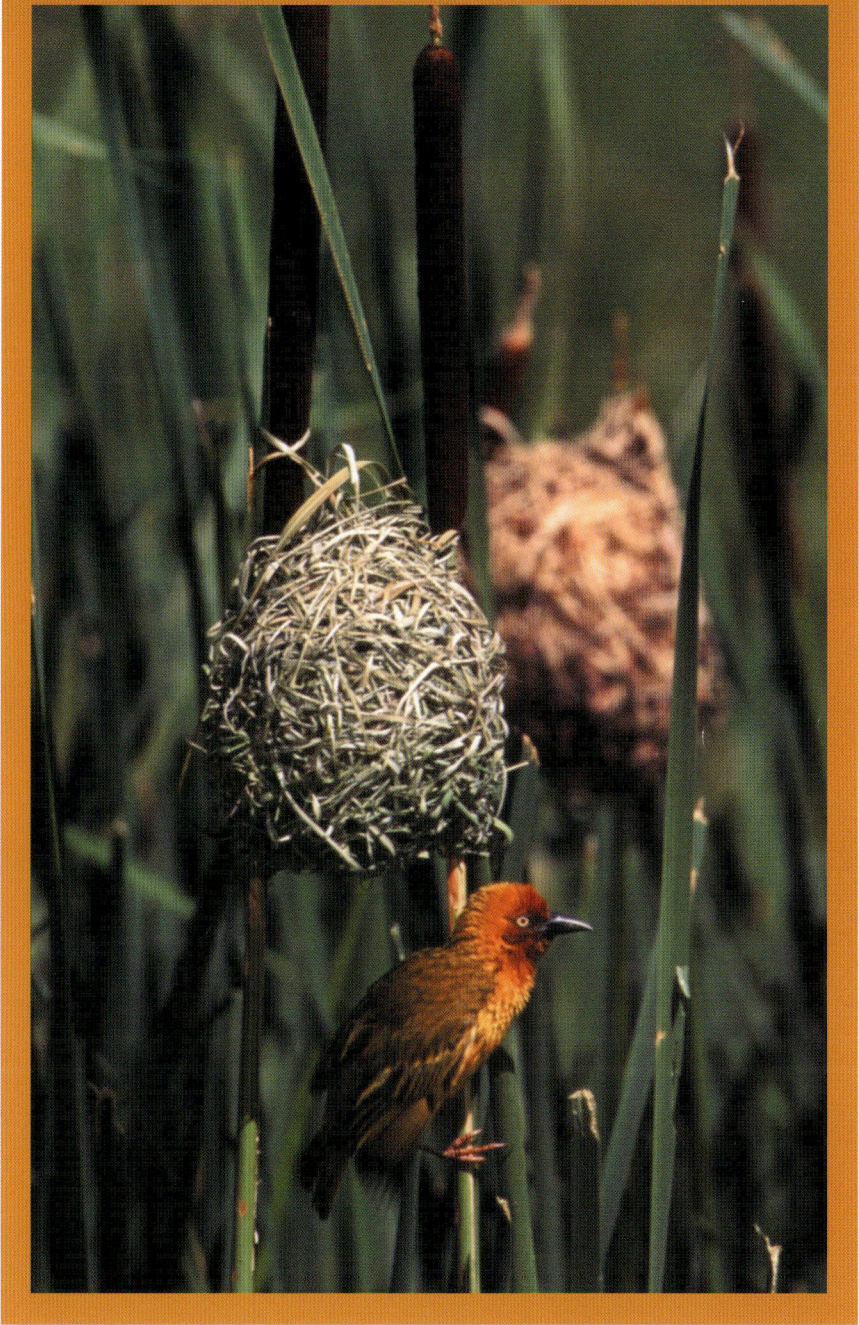

A weaverbird and its nest

We make safe places for animals to live and hide.

Zebras

We help the soil stay in place.
We have strong roots.

They wrap around soil or sand
and keep it from washing or
blowing away.

Animals nibble us.
People mow us.
Children play on us.

We are tough.

But we are tender
when we are new.

fun with phonics

How do we become fluent readers? We interpret, or decode, the written word. Knowledge of phonics—the rules and patterns for pronouncing letters—is essential. When we come upon a word we cannot figure out by any other strategy, we need to sound out that word.

Here are some very effective tools to help early readers along their way. Use the "add-on" technique to sound out unknown words. Simply add one sound at a time, always pronouncing previous sounds. For instance, to sound out the word **cat**, first say **c**, then **c-a**, then **c-a-t**, and finally the entire word **cat**. Reading "chunks" of letters is another important skill. These are patterns of two or more letters that make one sound.

Words from this book appear below. The markings are clues to help children master phonics rules and patterns. All consonant sounds are circled. Single vowels are either long –, short ˘, or silent /. Have fun with phonics, and a fluent reader will emerge.

If a vowel is followed by the letter "y," the "y" is a vowel. The two-vowels-together rule applies: the first vowel is long and says the letter name; the second vowel is silent.

s ā y   s t ā y   p l ā y

The "ow" letter combination can make either the long "o" sound or the "ou" sound that we make when we're hurt: OUCH!

g r ōw   h ŏ l l ōw   f l ōw

c ow s   m ōw

The "ing" letter combination will always say "ing," whether it is part of a word or fastened at the end (a suffix).

b l o͞o w ĭ n g   g r o͞o w ĭ n g   w ă s h ĭ n g

In the consonant cluster "wr," the "w" is silent.

w r ă p s

fun facts

- There are 6,000 to 10,000 different kinds of grasses.
- Bamboo is the tallest grass. One kind of bamboo grows as tall as a ten-story building.
- Grass grows from its base, not from the tip of its stem. That is why it keeps growing even after it has been mowed or grazed.
- All grasses have flowers, but grass flowers do not have petals.
- Some grasses are so beautiful that they are used in flower gardens. These are called ornamental grasses.

glossary/index

about the author

Anita Holmes is both a writer and an editor with a long career in children's and educational publishing. She has a special interest in nature, gardening, and the environment and has written numerous articles and books for children on these subjects. A number of her books have won commendations from the American Library Association, the National Science Teachers Association, and The New York Public Library. She lives in Norfolk, Connecticut.